THE GARDEN OF FEAR

BY

ROBERT E. HOWARD

British Library Cataloguing-in-Publication Data
A catalogue record for this book is available from the
British Library

Robert E. Howard

Robert Ervin Howard was born in Peaster, Texas in 1906. During his youth, his family moved between a variety of Texan boomtowns, and Howard – a bookish and somewhat introverted child – was steeped in the violent myths and legends of the Old South. Although he loved reading and learning, Howard developed a distinctly Texan, hardboiled outlook on the world. He became a passionate fan of boxing, taking it up at an amateur level, and from the age of nine began to write adventure tales of semi-historical bloodshed. In 1919, when Howard was thirteen, his family moved to the Central Texas hamlet of Cross Plains, where he would stay for the rest of his life.

At fifteen Howard began to read the pulp magazines of the day, and to write more seriously. The December 1922 issue of his high school newspaper featured two of his stories, 'Golden Hope Christmas' and 'West is West'. In 1924 he sold his first piece – a short caveman tale titled 'Spear and Fang' – for $16 to the not-yet-famous *Weird Tales* magazine. He published with the magazine regularly over the next few years. 1929 was a breakout year for Howard, in that the 23-year-old writer began to sell to other magazines, such as *Ghost Stories* and *Argosy*, both of whom had previously sent him hundreds of rejection slips. In 1930, he began a correspondence with weird fiction master H. P. Lovecraft which ran up to his death six years later, and is regarded as one of the great correspondence cycles in all of fantasy literature.

It was partly due to Lovecraft's encouragement that Howard created his most famous character, Conan the Cimmerian. Conan – a barbarian-turned-King during the Hyborian Age, a mythical period of some 12,000 years ago – featured in seventeen *Weird Tales* stories between 1933 and 1936, and is now regarded as having spawned the 'sword and sorcery' genre, making Howard's influence on fantasy literature comparable to that of J. R. R. Tolkien's. The Conan stories have since been adapted many times, most famously in the series of films starring Arnold Schwarzenegger.

Howard was enjoying an all-time high in sales by the beginning of 1936, but he was also deeply upset by the ill health of his mother, who had fallen into a coma. On the morning of June 11, 1936, he asked an attending nurse whether she would ever recover, and the nurse replied negatively. Howard walked to his car, parked outside the family home in Cross Plains, and shot himself. He died eight hours later, aged just thirty.

Once I was Hunwulf, the Wanderer. I cannot explain my knowledge of this fact by any occult or esoteric means, nor shall I try. A man remembers his past life; I remember my past _lives_. Just as a normal individual recalls the shapes that were him in childhood, boyhood and youth, so I recall the shapes that have been James Allison in forgotten ages. Why this memory is mine I cannot say, any more than I can explain the myriad other phenomena of nature which daily confront me and every other mortal. But as I lie waiting for death to free me from my long disease, I see with a clear, sure sight the grand panorama of lives that trail out behind me. I see the men who have been me, and I see the beasts that have been me.

For my memory does not end at the coming of Man. How could it, when the beast so shades into Man that there is no clearly divided line to mark the boundaries of bestiality? At this instant I see a dim twilight vista, among the gigantic trees of a primordial forest that never knew the tread of a leather-shod foot. I see a vast, shaggy, shambling bulk that lumbers clumsily yet swiftly, sometimes upright, sometimes on all fours. He delves under rotten logs for grubs and insects, and his small ears twitch continually. He lifts his head and bares yellow fangs. He is primordial, bestial, anthropoid; yet I recognize his kinship with the entity now called James Allison. Kinship? Say rather oneness. I am he;

he is I. My flesh is soft and white and hairless; his is dark and tough and shaggy. Yet we were one, and already in his feeble, shadowed brain are beginning to stir and tingle the man-thoughts and the man dreams, crude, chaotic, fleeting, yet the basis for all the high and lofty visions men have dreamed in all the following ages.

Nor does my knowledge cease there. It goes back, back, down immemorial vistas I dare not follow, to abysses too dark and awful for the human mind to plumb. Yet even there I am aware of my identity, my individuality. I tell you the individual is never lost, neither in the black pit from which we once crawled, blind, squalling and noisome, or in that eventual Nirvana in which we shall one day sink--which I have glimpsed afar off, shining as a blue twilight lake among the mountains of the stars.

But enough. I would tell you of Hunwulf. Oh, it was long, long ago! How long ago I dare not say. Why should I seek for paltry human comparisons to describe a realm indescribably, incomprehensibly distant? Since that age the earth had altered her contours not once but a dozen times, and whole cycles I of mankind have completed their destinies.

I was Hunwulf, a son of the golden-haired Aesir, who, from the icy plains of shadowy Asgard, sent I blue-eyed tribes around the world in century-long drifts to leave their trails in strange places. On one of those southward drifts I was born, for I never saw the homeland of my people, where the bulk of the Nordheimer still dwelt in their horse-hide tents among the snows.

I grew to manhood on that long wandering, to the fierce, sinewy, untamed manhood of the Aesir, who knew no gods but Ymir of the frost-rimmed beard, and whose axes are stained with the blood of many nations. My thews were like woven steel cords. My yellow hair fell in a lion-like mane to my mighty shoulders. My loins were girt with leopard skin. With either hand I could wield my heavy flint-headed axe. Year by year my tribe drifted southward, sometimes swinging in long arcs to east or west, sometimes lingering for months or years in fertile valleys or plains where the grass-eaters swarmed, but always forging slowly and inevitably southward. Sometimes our way led through vast and breathless solitudes that had never known a human cry; sometimes strange tribes disputed our course, and our trail passed over bloodstained ashes of butchered villages. And amidst this wandering, hunting and slaughtering, I came to full manhood and the love of Gudrun.

What shall I say of Gudrun? How describe color to the blind? I can say that her skin was whiter than milk, that her hair was living gold with the flame of the sun caught in it, that the supple beauty other body would shame the dream that shaped the Grecian goddesses. But I cannot make you realize the fire and wonder that was Gudrun. You have no basis for comparison; you know womanhood only by the women of your epoch, who, beside her are like candles beside the glow of the full moon. Not for a millennium of millenniums have women like Gudrun walked the earth. Cleopatra, Thais, Helen of Troy, they were but pallid shadows of her beauty, frail mimicries of the blossom that blooms to full glory only in the primordial.

For Gudrun I forsook my tribe and my people, and went into the wilderness, an exile and an outcast, with blood on my hands. She was of my race, but not of my tribe: a waif whom we found as a child wandering in a dark forest, lost from some wandering tribe of our blood. She grew up in the tribe, and when she came to the full ripeness of her glorious young womanhood, she was given to Heimdul the Strong, the mightiest hunter of the tribe.

But the dream of Gudrun was madness in my soul, a flame that burned eternally, and for her I slew Heimdul, crushing his skull with my flint-headed axe ere he could bear her to his horse-hide tent. And then follows our long flight from the vengeance of the tribe. Willingly she went with me, for she loved me with the love of the Aesir women, which is a devouring flame that destroys weakness. Oh, it was a savage age, when life was grim and bloodstained, and the weak died quickly. There was nothing mild or gentle about us, our passions were those of the tempest, the surge and impact of battle, the challenge of the lion. Our loves were as terrible as our hates.

And so I carried Gudrun from the tribe, and the killers were hot on our trail. For a night and a day they pressed us hard, until we swam a rising river, a roaring, foaming torrent that even the men of the Aesir dared not attempt. But in the madness of our love and recklessness we buffetted our way across, beaten and torn by the frenzy of the flood, and reached the farther bank alive.

Then for many days we traversed upland forests haunted by tigers and leopards, until we came to a great barrier of mountains, blue ramparts climbing awesomely to the sky. Slope piled upon slope.

In those mountains we were assailed by freezing winds and hunger, and by giant condors which swept down upon us with a thunder of gigantic wings. In grim battles in the passes I shot away all my arrows and splintered my flintheaded spear, but at last we crossed the bleak backbone of the range and descending the southern slopes, came upon a village of mud huts among the cliffs inhabited by a peaceful, brown-skinned people who spoke a strange tongue and had strange customs. But they greeted us with the sign of peace, and brought us into their village, where they set meat and barley-bread and fermented milk before us, and squatted in a ring about us while we ate, and a woman slapped softly on a bowl-shaped tom-tom to do us honor.

We had reached their village at dusk, and night fell while we feasted. On all sides rose the cliffs and peaks shouldering massively against the stars. The little cluster of mud huts and the tiny fires were drowned and lost in the immensity of the night. Gudrun felt the loneliness, the crowding desolation of that darkness, and she pressed close to me, her shoulder against my breast. But my axe was close at my hand, and I had never known the sensation of fear.

The little brown people squatted before us, men and women, and tried to talk to us with motions of their slender hands. Dwelling always in one place, in comparative security, they lacked both the strength and the uncompromising ferocity of the nomadic Aesir. Their hands fluttered with friendly gestures in the firelight.

I made them understand that we had come from the north, had crossed the backbone of the great mountain range, and that on the morrow it was our intention to descend into the green tablelands which we had glimpsed southward of the peaks. When they understood my meaning they set up a great cry shaking their heads violently, and beating madly on the drum. They were all so eager to impart something to me, and all waving their hands at once, that they bewildered rather than enlightened me. Eventually they did make me understand that they did not wish me to descend the mountains. Some menace lay to the south of the village, but whether of man or beast, I could not learn.

It was while they were all gesticulating and my whole attention was centered on their gestures, that the blow fell. The first intimation was a sudden thunder of wings in my ears; a dark shape rushed out of the night, and a great pinion dealt me a buffet over the head as I turned. I was knocked sprawling, and in that instant I heard Gudrun scream as she was torn from my side. Bounding up, quivering with a furious eagerness to rend and slay, I saw the dark shape vanish again into the darkness, a white, screaming, writhing figure trailing from its talons.

Roaring my grief and fury I caught up my axe and charged into the dark--then halted short, wild, desperate, knowing not which way to turn.

The little brown people had scattered, screaming, knocking sparks from their fires as they rushed over them in their haste to gain their huts, but now they crept out fearfully, whimpering like wounded dogs. They gathered around me and plucked at me with timid hands and chattered in their tongue while I cursed in sick impotency, knowing they wished to tell me something which I could not understand.

At last I suffered them to lead me back to the fire, and there the oldest man of the tribe brought forth a strip of cured hide, a clay pot of pigments, and a stick. On the hide he painted a crude picture of a winged thing carrying a white woman--oh, it was very crude, but I made out his meaning. Then all pointed southward and cried out loudly in their own tongue; and I knew that the menace they had warned me against was the thing that had carried off Gudrun. Until then I supposed that it had been one of the great mountain condors which had carried her away, but the picture the old man drew, in black paint, resembled a winging man more than anything else.

Then, slowly and laboriously, he began to trace something I finally recognized as a map--oh, yes, even in those dim days we had our primitive maps, though no modern man would be able to comprehend them so greatly different was our symbolism.

It took a long time; it was midnight before the old man had finished and I understood his tracings. But at last the matter was made clear. If I followed the course traced on the map, down the long narrow valley where stood the village, across a plateau, down a series of rugged slopes and along another valley, I would come to the place where lurked the being which had stolen my woman. At that spot the old man drew what looked like a mis-shapen hut, with many strange markings all about it in red pigments. Pointing to these, and again to me, he shook his head, with those loud cries that seemed to indicate peril among these people.

Then they tried to persuade me not to go, but afire with eagerness I took the piece of hide and pouch of food they thrust into my hands (they were indeed a strange people for that age), grasped my axe and set off in the moonless

10

darkness. But my eyes were keener than a modern mind can comprehend, and my sense of direction was as a wolfs. Once the map was fixed in my mind, I could have thrown it away and come unerring to the place I sought but I folded it and thrust it into my girdle.

I traveled at my best speed through the starlight, taking no heed of any beasts that might be seeking their prey- -cave bear or saber-toothed tiger. At times I heard gravel slide under stealthy padded paws; I glimpsed fierce yellow eyes burning in the darkness, and caught sight of shadowy, skulking forms. But I plunged on recklessly, in too desperate a mood to give the path to any beast however fearsome.

I traversed the valley, climbed a ridge and came out on a broad plateau, gashed with ravines and strewn with boulders. I crossed this and in the darkness before dawn commenced my climb down the treacherous slopes. They seemed endless, falling away in a long steep incline until their feet were lost in darkness. But I went down recklessly, not pausing to unsling the rawhide rope I carried about my shoulders, trusting to my luck and skill to bring me down without a broken neck.

And just as dawn was touching the peaks with a white glow, I dropped into a broad valley, walled by stupendous cliffs. At that point it was wide from east to west, but the cliffs converged toward the lower end, giving the valley the appearance of a great fan, narrowing swiftly toward the south.

The floor was level, traversed by a winding stream. Trees grew thinly; there was no underbrush, but a carpet of tall grass, which at that time of year were somewhat dry. Along the stream where the green lush grew, wandered mammoths, hairy mountains of flesh and muscle.

I gave them a wide berth, giants too mighty for me to cope with, confident in their power, and afraid of only one thing on earth. They bent forward their great ears and lifted their trunks menacingly when I approached too near, but they did not attack me. I ran swiftly among the trees, and the sun was not yet above the eastern ramparts which its rising edged with golden flame, when I came to the point where the cliffs converged. My night-long climb had not affected my iron muscles. I felt no weariness; my fury burned unabated. What lay beyond the cliffs I could not know; I ventured no conjecture. I had room in my brain only for red wrath and killing-lust.

The cliffs did not form a solid wall. That is, the extremities of the converging palisades did not meet, leaving a notch or gap a few hundred feet wide, and emerged into a second valley, or rather into a continuance of the same valley which broadened out again beyond the pass.

The cliffs slanted away swiftly to east and west, to form a giant rampart that marched clear around the valley in the shape of a vast oval. It formed a blue rim all around the valley without a break except for a glimpse of the clear sky that seemed to mark another notch at the southern end. The inner valley was shaped much like a great bottle, with two necks.

The neck by which I entered was crowded with trees, which grew densely for several hundred yards, when they gave way abruptly to a field of crimson flowers. And a few hundred yards beyond the edges of the trees, I saw a strange structure.

I must speak of what I saw not alone as Hunwulf, but as James Allison as well. For Hunwulf only vaguely comprehended the things he saw, and, as Hunwulf, he could not describe them at all. I, as Hunwulf, knew nothing of architecture. The only man-built dwelling I had ever seen had been the horse-hide tents of my people, and the thatched mud huts of the barley people--and other people equally primitive.

So as Hunwulf I could only say that I looked upon a great hut the construction of which was beyond my comprehension. But I, James Allison, know that it was a tower, some seventy feet in height, of a curious green stone, highly polished, and of a substance that created the illusion of semi-translucency. It was cylindrical, and, as near as I could see, without doors or windows. The main body of the building was perhaps sixty feet in height, and from its center rose a smaller tower that completed its full stature. This tower, being much inferior in girth to the main body of the structure, and thus surrounded by a sort of gallery, with a crenellated parapet, and was furnished with both doors, curiously arched, and windows, thickly barred as I could see, even from where I stood.

That was all. No evidence of human occupancy. No sign of life in all the valley. But it was evident that this castle was what the old man of the mountain village had been trying to draw, and I was certain that in it I would find Gudrun--if she still lived.

Beyond the tower I saw the glimmer of a blue lake into which the stream, following the curve of the western wall, eventually flowed. Lurking amid the trees I glared at the tower and at the flowers surrounding it on all sides, growing thick along the walls and extending for hundreds of yards in all directions. There were trees at the other end of the valley, near the lake; but no trees grew among the flowers.

They were not like any plants I had ever seen. They grew close together, almost touching each other. They were some four feet in height, with only one blossom on each stalk, a blossom larger than a man's head, with broad, fleshy petals drawn close together. These petals were a livid crimson, the hue of an open wound. The stalks were thick as a man's wrist, colorless, almost transparent. The poisonously green leaves were shaped like spearheads, drooping on long snaky stems.

Their whole aspect was repellent, and I wondered what their denseness concealed.

For all my wild-born instincts were roused in me. I felt lurking peril, just as I had often sensed the ambushed lion before my external senses recognized him. I scanned the dense blossoms closely, wondering if some great serpent lay coiled among them. My nostrils expanded as I quested for a scent, but the wind was blowing away from me. But there was something decidedly unnatural about that vast garden. Though the north wind swept over it, not a blossom stirred, not a leaf rustled; they hung motionless, sullen, like birds of prey with drooping heads, and I had a strange feeling that they were watching me like living things.

It was like a landscape in a dream: on either hand the blue cliffs lifting against the cloud-fleeced sky; in the distance the dreaming lake; and that fantastic green tower rising in the midst of that livid crimson field.

And there was something else: in spite of the wind that was blowing away from me, I caught a scent, a charnel-house reek of death and decay and corruption that rose from the blossoms.

Then suddenly I crouched closer in my covert. There was life and movement on the castle. A figure emerged from the tower, and coming to the parapet, leaned upon it and looked out across the valley. It was a man, but such a man as I had never dreamed of, even in nightmares.

He was tall, powerful, black with the hue of polished ebony; but the feature which made a human nightmare of him was the batlike wings which folded on his shoulders. I knew they were wings: the fact was obvious and indisputable.

I, James Allison, have pondered much on that phenomenon which I witnessed through the eyes of Hunwulf. Was that winged man merely a freak, an isolated example of distorted nature, dwelling in solitude and immemorial desolation? Or was he a survival of a forgotten race, which had risen, reigned and vanished before the coming of man as we know him? The little brown people of the hills might have told me, but we had no speech in common. Yet I am inclined to the latter theory. Winged men are not uncommon in mythology; they are met with in the folklore of many nations and many races. As far back as man may go in myth, chronicle and legend, he finds tales of harpies and winged gods, angels and demons. Legends are distorted shadows of pre-existent realities, I believe that once a race of winged black men ruled a pre-Adamite world, and that I, Hunwulf, met the last survivor of that race in the valley of the red blossoms.

These thoughts I think as James Allison, with my modern knowledge which is as imponderable as my modern ignorance.

I, Hunwulf, indulged in no such speculations. Modern skepticism was not a part of my nature, nor did

I seek to rationalize what seemed not to coincide with a natural universe. I acknowledged no gods but Ymir and his daughters, but I did not doubt the existence--as demons--of other deities, worshipped by other races. Supernatural beings of all sorts fitted into my conception of life and the universe. I no more doubted the existence of dragons, ghosts, fiends and devils than I doubted the existence of lions and buffaloes and elephants. I accepted this freak of nature as a supernatural demon and did not worry about its origin or source. Nor was I thrown into a panic of superstitious fear. I was a son of Asgard, who feared neither man nor devil, and I had more faith in the crushing power of my flint axe than in the spells of priests or the incantations of sorcerers.

But I did not immediately rush into the open and charge the tower. The wariness of the wild was mine, and I saw no way to climb the castle. The winged man needed no doors on the side, because he evidently entered at the top, and the slick surface of the walls seemed to defy the most skillful climber. Presently a way of getting upon the tower occurred to me, but I hesitated, waiting to see if any other winged people appeared, though I had an unexplainable feeling that he was the only one of his kind in the valley--possibly in the world. While I crouched among the trees and watched, I saw him lift his elbows from the parapet and stretch lithely, like a great cat. Then he strode across the circular gallery and entered the tower. A muffled cry rang out on the air which caused me to stiffen, though even so I realized that it was not the cry of a woman. Presently the black master of the castle emerged, dragging a smaller figure with him--a figure which writhed and struggled and cried out piteously. I saw that it was a small brown man, much like those of the mountain village. Captured, I did not doubt, as Gudrun had been captured.

He was like a child in the hands of his huge foe. The black man spread broad wings and rose over the parapet, carrying his captive as a condor might carry a sparrow. He soared out over the field of blossoms, while I crouched in my leafy retreat, glaring in amazement.

The winged man, hovering in mid-air, voiced a strange weird cry; and it was answered in horrible fashion. A shudder of awful life passed over the crimson field beneath him. The great red blossoms trembled, opened, spreading their fleshy petals like the mouths of serpents. Their stalks seemed to elongate, stretching upward eagerly. Their broad leaves lifted and vibrated with a curious lethal whirring, like the singing of a rattlesnake. A faint but flesh-crawling hissing sounded over all the valley. The blossoms gasped, straining upward. And with a fiendish laugh, the winged man dropped his writhing captive.

With a scream of a lost soul the brown man hurtled downward, crashing among the flowers. And with a rustling hiss, they were on him. Their thick flexible stalks arched like the necks of serpents, their petals closed on his flesh. A hundred blossoms clung to him like the tentacles of an octopus, smothering and crushing him down. His shrieks of agony came muffled; he was completely hidden by the hissing, threshing flowers. Those beyond reach swayed and writhed furiously as if seeking to tear up their roots in their eagerness to join their brothers. All over the field the great red blossoms leaned and strained toward the spot where the grisly battle went on. The shrieks sank lower and lower and lower, and ceased. A dread silence reigned over the valley. The black man flapped his way leisurely back to the tower, and vanished within it.

Then presently the blossoms detached themselves one by one from their victim who lay very white and still. Aye, his whiteness was more than that of death; he was like a wax image, a staring effigy from which every drop of blood had been sucked. And a startling transmutation was evident in the flowers directly about him. Their stalks no longer colorless; they were swollen and dark red, like transparent bamboos filled to the bursting with fresh blood.

Drawn by an insatiable curiosity, I stole from the trees and glided to the very edge of the red field. The blossoms hissed and bent toward me, spreading their petals like the hood of a roused cobra. Selecting one farthest from its brothers, I severed the stalk with a stroke of my axe, and the thing tumbled to the ground, writhing like a beheaded serpent.

When its struggles ceased I bent over it in wonder. The stalk was not hollow as I had supposed--that is, hollow like a dry bamboo. It was traversed by a network of thread-like veins, some empty and some exuding a colorless sap. The stems which held the leaves to the stalk were remarkably tenacious and pliant, and the leaves themselves were edged with curved spines, like sharp hooks.

Once those spines were sunk in the flesh, the victim would be forced to tear up the whole plant by the roots if he escaped.

The petals were each as broad as my hand, and as thick as a prickly pear, and on the inner side covered with innumerable tiny mouths, not larger than the head of a pin. In the center, where the pistil should be, there was a barbed spike, of a substance like thorn, and narrow channels between the four serrated edges.

From my investigations of this horrible travesty of vegetation, I looked up suddenly, just in time to see the winged man appear again on the parapet. He did not seem particularly surprised to see me. He shouted in his unknown tongue and made a mocking gesture, while I stood statue-like, gripping my axe. Presently he turned and entered the tower as he had done before; and as before, he emerged with a captive. My fury and hate were almost submerged by the flood of joy that Gudrun was alive.

In spite of her supple strength, which was that of a she-panther, the black man handled Gudrun as easily as he had handled the brown man. Lifting her struggling white body high above his head, he displayed her to me and yelled tauntingly. Her golden hair streamed over her white shoulders as she fought vainly, crying to me in the terrible extremity of her fright and horror. Not lightly was a woman of the Aesir reduced to cringing terror. I measured the depths of her captor's diabolism by her frenzied cries.

But I stood motionless. If it would have saved her, I would have plunged into that crimson morass of hell, to be hooked and pierced and sucked white by those fiendish flowers. But that would help her none. My death would merely leave her without a defender. So I stood silent while she writhed and whimpered, and the black man's laughter sent red waves of madness surging across my brain. Once he made as if to cast her down among the flowers, and my iron control almost snapped and sent me plunging into that red sea of hell. But it was only a gesture. Presently he dragged her back to the tower and tossed her inside. Then he turned back to the parapet, rested his elbows upon it, and fell to watching me. Apparently he was playing with us as a cat plays with a mouse before he destroys it.

But while he watched, I turned my back and strode into the forest. I, Hunwulf, was not a thinker, as modern men understand the term. I lived in an age where emotions were translated by the smash of a flint axe rather than by emanations of the intellect. Yet I was not the senseless animal the black man evidently supposed me to be. I had a human brain, whetted by the eternal struggle for existence and supremacy.

I knew I could not cross that red strip that banded the castle, alive. Before I could take a half dozen steps a score of barbed spikes would be thrust into my flesh, their avid mouths sucking the flood from my veins to feed their demoniac lust. Even my tigerish strength would not avail to hew a path through them.

The winged man did not follow. Looking back, I saw him still lounging in the same position. When I, as James Allison, dream again the dreams of Hunwulf, that, image is etched in my mind, that gargoyle figure with elbows propped on the parapet, like a medieval devil brooding on the battlements of hell.

I passed through the straits of the valley and came into the vale beyond where the trees thinned and the mammoths lumbered along the stream. Beyond the herd I stopped and drawing a pair of flints into my pouch, stooped and struck a spark in the dry grass. Running swiftly from chosen place to place, I set a dozen fires, in a great semi-circle. The north wind caught them, whipped them into eager life, drove them before it. In a few moments a rampart of flame was sweeping down the valley.

The mammoths ceased their feeding, lifted their great ears and bellowed alarm. In all the world they feared only fire. They began to retreat southward, the cows herding the calves before them, bulls trumpeting like the blast of Judgement Day. Roaring like a storm the fire rushed on, and the mammoths broke and stampeded, a crushing hurricane of flesh, a thundering earthquake of hurtling bone and muscle. Trees splintered and went down before them, the ground shook under their headlong tread. Behind them came the racing fire and on the heels of the fire came I, so closely that the smouldering earth burnt the moose-hide sandals off my feet.

Through the narrow neck they thundered, levelling the dense thickets like a giant scythe. Trees were torn up by the roots; it was as if a tornado had ripped through the pass.

With a deafening thunder of pounding feet and trumpeting, they stormed across the sea of red blossoms. Those devilish plants might have even pulled down and destroyed a single mammoth; but under the impact of the whole herd, they were no more than common flowers. The maddened titans crashed through and over them, battering them to shreds, hammering, stamping them into the earth which grew soggy with their juice.

I trembled for an instant, fearing the brutes would not turn aside for the castle, and dubious of even it being able to withstand that battering ram concussion. Evidently the winged man shared my fears, for he shot up from the tower and raced off through the sky toward the lake. But one of the bulls butted head-on into the wall, was shunted off the smooth curving surface, caromed into the one next to him, and the herd split and roared by the tower on either hand, so closely their hairy sides rasped against it. They thundered on through the red field toward the distant lake.

The fire, reaching the edge of the trees, was checked; the smashed sappy fragments of the red flowers would not burn. Trees, fallen or standing, smoked and burst into flame, and burning branches showered around me as I ran through the trees and out into the gigantic swath the charging herd had cut through the livid field.

As I ran I shouted to Gudrun and she answered me. Her voice was muffled and accompanied by a hammering on something. The winged man had locked her in a tower.

As I came under the castle wall, treading on remnants of red petals and snaky stalks, I unwound my rawhide rope, swung it, and sent its loop shooting upward to catch on one of the merlons of the crenellated parapet. Then I went up it, hand over hand, gripping the rope between my toes, bruising my knuckles and elbows against the sheer wall as I swung about.

I was within five feet of the parapet when I was galvanized by the beat of wings about my head. The black man shot out of the air and landed on the gallery. I got a good look at him as he leaned over the parapet. His features were straight and regular; there was no suggestion of the negroid about him. His eyes were slanted slits, and his teeth gleamed in a savage grin of hate and triumph. Long, long he had ruled the valley of the red blossoms, levelling tribute of human lives from the miserable tribes of the hills, for writhing victims to feed the carnivorous half-bestial flowers which were his subjects and protectors. And now I was in his power, my fierceness, and craft gone for naught. A stroke of the crooked dagger in his hand and I would go hurtling to my death. Somewhere Gudrun, seeing my peril, was screaming like a wild thing, and then a door crashed with a splintering of wood.

The black man, intent upon his gloating, laid the keen edge of his dagger on the rawhide strand--then a strong white arm locked about his neck from behind, and he was jerked violently backward. Over his shoulder I saw the beautiful face of Gudrun, her hair standing on end, her eyes dilated with terror and fury.

With a roar he turned in her grasp, tore loose her clinging arms and hurled her against the tower with such force that she lay half stunned. Then he turned again to me, but in that instant I had swarmed up and over the parapet, and leaped upon the gallery, unslinging my axe.

For an instant he hesitated, his wings half-lifted, his hand poising on his dagger, as if uncertain whether to fight or take to the air. He was a giant in stature, with muscles standing out in corded ridges all over him, but he hesitated, as uncertain as a man when confronted by a wild beast.

I did not hesitate. With a deep-throated roar I sprang, swinging my axe with all my giant strength. With a strangled cry he threw up his arms; but down between them the axe plunged and blasted his head to red ruin.

I wheeled toward Gudrun; and struggling to her knees, she threw her white arms about me in a desperate clasp of love and terror, staring awedly to where lay the winged lord of the valley, the crimson pulp that had been his head drowned in a puddle of blood and brains.

I had often wished that it were possible to draw these various lives of mine together in one body, combining the experiences of Hunwulf with the knowledge of James Allison. Could that be so, Hunwulf would have gone through the ebony door which Gudrun in her desperate strength had shattered, into that weird chamber he glimpsed through the ruined panels, with fantastic furnishing, and shelves heaped with rolls of parchment. He would have unrolled those scrolls and pored over their characters until he deciphered them, and read, perhaps, the chronicles of that weird race whose last survivor he had just slain. Surely the tale was stranger than an opium dream, and marvelous as the story of lost Atlantis.

But Hunwulf had no such curiosity. To him the tower, the ebony furnished chamber and the rolls of parchment were meaningless, inexplicable emanations of sorcery, whose significance lay only in their diabolism. Though the solution of mystery lay under his fingers, he was a far removed from it as James Allison, millenniums yet unborn.

To me, Hunwulf, the castle was but a monstrous trap, concerning which I had but one emotion, and that a desire to escape from it as quickly as possible.

With Gudrun clinging to me I slid to the ground, then with a dextrous flip I freed my rope and wound it; and after that we went hand and hand along the path made by the mammoths, now vanishing in the distance, toward the blue lake at the southern end of the valley and the notch in the cliffs beyond it.

THE END